Signal's
Airport
Adventure

by Stormy Friday
Illustrations by Phyllis Saroff

ISBN: 0-9717047-5-9

Tails From
Friday Harbor

Read Aloud to Me Book

http://www.tailsfromfridayharbor.com

Published by Bay Media, Inc.
550M Ritchie Highway, #271
Severna Park, MD 21146
Tel: 410-647-8402 · Fax: 410-544-4640
Web site: www.baymed.com

Dedication

*To my two-legged
and
four-legged family!*

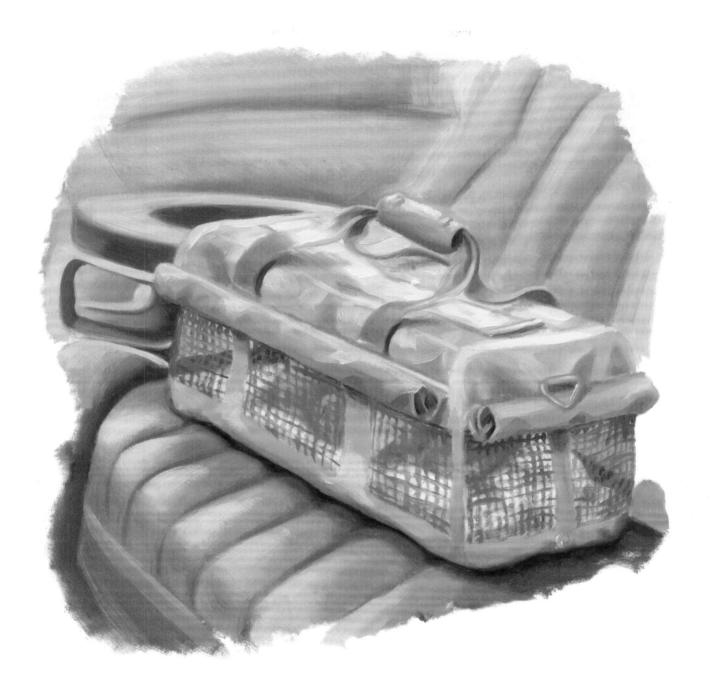

Two tiny, gray kittens lie in a carrier in the back seat of a car. The car is headed to an airport where the kitties will ride on a plane with their new mom and dad to a place they've never been before. Their new home is called Friday Harbor, and it's on a large river called the Magothy.

Telegraph is the girl kitten. She is small, light gray, and has a round, doll-like face. She has a short, bushy tail that is much too big for her little body.

Her brother, Signal, is bigger than his sister and much darker gray. He has a long, thin tail that forms a question mark when he walks. He also has big ears. Both kittens have amber eyes that get brighter every day.

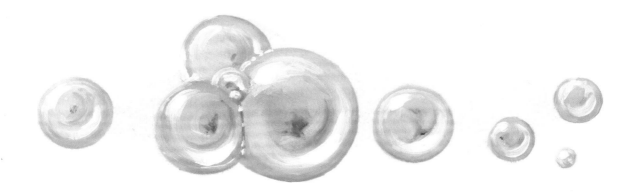

"Today is the first day of our new life," Signal said to his sister. Then he repeated his name. "Signal, Signal, Signal," he said boldly. "I like the name our new human mom and dad gave me."

"I like my name too," said Telegraph, grinning at her brother. "What do you suppose our names mean?"

"I don't know, but I like our new human mom and dad; they smell good and are very friendly. Our new human mom gives good kisses and our dad has a funny laugh." Signal thought for a minute, "Maybe our names have something to do with water. I heard them say we are going to live *in* the Magothy River. Do you think we'll always be wet?"

"Not *in* the water…*on* the water silly," said Telegraph with a smirk, "…and I don't think our names have anything to do with water. I also heard them say they have an old cat named Annie who will be our Auntie. I hope she licks our fur and tells us stories. We'll have to ask her about our names."

Signal was focused on the topic of water and disregarded Telegraph's comments about Auntie Annie. "What do you think we should call our new human mom and dad?" he asked. "We need to give them names, too. I think they need water names. What do you think about Miss Splash and Mr. Bubbles? They are water names. Remember, humans like to take bubble baths and splash around in the water. Miss Splash and Mr. Bubbles are good water names."

"You are so clever Signal," said Telegraph. "Those are perfect names. Now it's settled. We have new names and so do they. What a good start to our new life!"

The airport was hustling and bustling when the car pulled up in front of it. There were loud voices, and the kittens were frightened.

"I didn't know there were so many humans," said Signal. "They sure are noisy."

Signal stood up to move closer to Telegraph and let out a little "yelp."

"What's wrong?" asked Telegraph.

"I get a sharp pain in my left rear paw when I stand on it," Signal replied. "I can't see anything in it, but it hurts a lot."

"I wonder what it could be," said Telegraph, as they snuggled tightly together.

Signal reached over and put his paw around Telegraph's neck. "I'm glad I'm not alone in this carrier."

Telegraph licked Signal's ear and said softly, "Me too, Signal."

After waiting in a long line, the humans and the kittens reached the security area where the humans took off their shoes and put them in boxes. Other humans, in front and back of them, were doing the same thing. The many boxes moved forward on a funny looking black rubber table and disappeared into a black hole. Miss Splash put her pocketbook in a box, too. Then Mr. Bubbles emptied his pockets, dumping change, a cell phone, two pens, and a few paper clips into another box. Telegraph and Signal exchanged glances at this strange sight.

"What is happening, Telegraph?" asked Signal. "Are they going to take their clothes off, too? Do you think we have to go in one of those boxes on the moving thing that goes through the machine? It sure makes weird sounds."

"I hope not," replied Telegraph. "It looks dark and scary in there."

Next, a man in a uniform stopped the black moving table and called out to Telegraph's mom and dad.

"Well, well, what do we have here? Little kittens?" he asked. "They have to come out of that carrier, and each of you has to hold one while you walk through the metal detector."

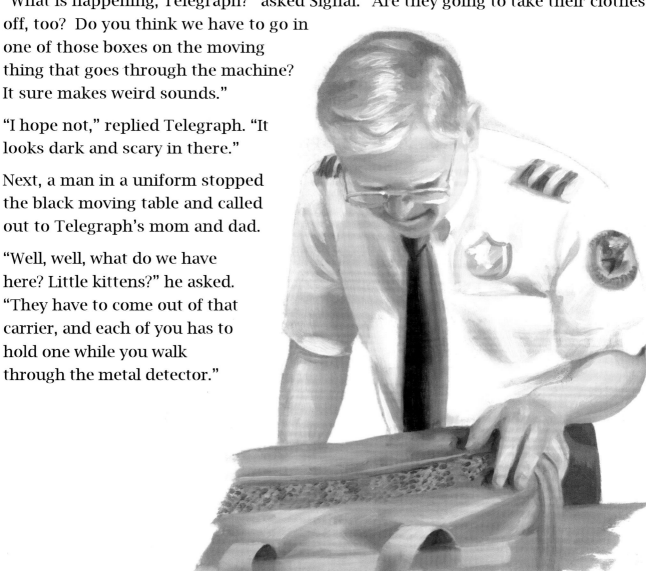

Telegraph and Signal hugged each other in the carrier, as they looked over at the other funny looking machine. Miss Splash said to the man, "They are really scared, so give us a minute to get them out of the carrier."

She placed the carrier on a table behind the moving rubber thing and opened the door slowly.

"I'm not going through that thing," Signal said to Telegraph. "Listen to the noise it makes when some humans go through it." Signal moved to the very back of the carrier and crouched low.

Miss Splash reached in and gently lifted Telegraph out. Signal started to cry. "It is going to be okay, Signal. Miss Splash won't let it hurt us," said Telegraph. "Don't worry. Just watch me do it."

Cradling Telegraph in her arms, Miss Splash walked slowly through the metal detector. Nothing happened.

"You can do it!" she called back to her brother, as Mr. Bubbles reached in and tried to pull Signal out.

Mr. Bubbles struggled to get Signal out of the carrier. Other humans behind him waited impatiently for the two of them to go through. The line wasn't moving. Signal was hugging the back of the carrier and howling at the top of his lungs. Everyone stopped and looked to see what was happening.

"I'm not coming out!" wailed Signal.

"Stop it, Signal," Telegraph snapped back at her brother. "Look at the problems you are causing! Just let Mr. Bubbles get you out and stop whining."

Signal crept toward the front of the carrier, where Mr. Bubbles caught him and pulled him out. Poor Signal stiffened up so that all four of his legs were sticking straight out in different directions. Everyone in line laughed at him, and so did the security men. Signal felt annoyed that everyone always laughed at him, while his sister sailed through things easily and then scolded him.

Mr. Bubbles walked slowly up to the metal detector and through it. All of a sudden, bells and whistles started blaring from the machine. Signal started howling again.

"You'll have to step over here so we can put the wand on you and see what the problem is," said the man in uniform. Pointing to Mr. Bubbles, he asked, "Sir, do you have any other metal on you?" Mr. Bubbles was certain he'd put all his metal in the moving boxes.

Miss Splash had put Telegraph back in the carrier. The kitten pushed on the mesh at the front of the carrier straining to see what was happening.

"Stop crying, Signal," she said. "Everything will be OK. And relax your legs. You look like an octopus. Mr. Bubbles can't even hold you."

A uniformed man told Mr. Bubbles to stand in a certain spot and hold the trembling Signal away from his body. The man ran the wand around Mr. Bubbles from top to bottom, and nothing happened. Then he ran the wand around Signal's body, and the wand started making all kinds of noises.

"It's the kitten," the man said.

Signal looked at Telegraph, "What are they saying? What are they going to do to me now?"

"I can't imagine what the problem is," said Mr. Bubbles to the security guard. "We just got these kittens, and they have been in their carrier the whole time."

The security man wanted to run the wand over Signal more thoroughly and pointed to another table where Mr. Bubbles was gently placing Signal and talking softly to him.

Miss Splash brought over the carrier with Telegraph inside. Signal still had his legs stretched out, so he was spread out on the table. He looked at his sister, unable to speak. His amber eyes were wide with fear.

First, the security man picked Signal up. He put the wand to Signal's right front paw. Nothing happened. Next, he did the left front paw, and nothing happened. He put the wand on the right rear paw, and still nothing. As he approached the left rear paw, the wand started making a loud noise.

Miss Splash and Telegraph both gasped.

"What do we have here?" said the security guard. As the man took Signal's paw to look between his toes, Signal felt a sharp pain and let out a loud "Meeeee....... ooooooooooowww!"

The security guard looked closer and saw something wedged in between two of Signal's toes. "Look at this!" he said to Mr. Bubbles. "There is a little metal bead in there."

Pulling a magnifying glass and some tweezers from his pocket, the man spread Signal's toes and carefully grabbed the little bead. "It looks like a bead from a necklace or bracelet," he said, showing the bead to Mr. Bubbles and Miss Splash. "He must have stepped on it."

Signal stopped crying immediately and looked at Telegraph. "I know what happened," he said with a satisfied look on his face. "Remember when that necklace broke yesterday and dropped on the floor? We all chased the beads and had so much fun. I must have stepped on one of them and didn't know it." He looked thoughtfully at his paw as he stretched it, "No wonder my paw hurt a bit when I stepped down hard on it."

"Thanks for being so cooperative, little fellow," said the security man as he reached into the cage and scratched Signal under his chin. "You take care now."

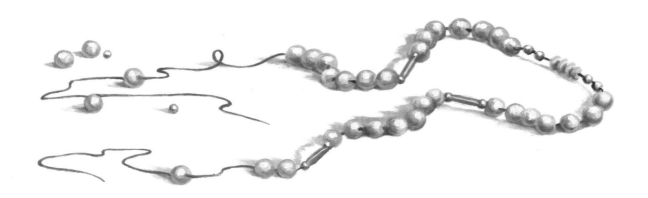

By the time they got to the gate area, Miss Splash, Mr. Bubbles, and the kittens were tired from their ordeal at security.

Miss Splash looked at Mr. Bubbles. "I can't wait to get home, get these little ones settled, and crawl into bed," she said. "We've been up for a long time." Mr. Bubbles nodded at her, then quickly looked away as he heard the gate agent say something about their flight to another passenger.

"Flight 762 to Baltimore is going to be delayed three hours due to bad weather where the plane is coming from," the gate agent said. Mr. Bubbles and Miss Splash exchanged worried glances. They clearly were upset.

"Now what is the problem?" Signal asked Telegraph. "I couldn't understand what that human was saying, but Miss Splash and Mr. Bubbles don't look very happy."

"Something about our plane," Telegraph replied.

"Three hours!" Miss Splash said to Mr. Bubbles. "These poor babies need to get to their new home. They must be tired, hungry, and thirsty. I'm glad we got some dry food for the trip."

"Why don't you go sit down, and I'll find some water for them," Mr. Bubbles said gently, pointing to a seat.

Miss Splash sat down just as Signal started whining. "I'm hot and tired," he said to Telegraph. "I need some food, and I'm very thirsty," he squealed.

"Signal, stop complaining," Telegraph said sternly. "You don't want Miss Splash and Mr. Bubbles to think we have bad manners. They can't help what is happening with the plane. Besides, we have food, and Mr. Bubbles is getting us some water."

"I'm so hot," he said, "and I don't like being stuck in this carrier."

Hearing all the kitten noises, Miss Splash unzipped the top of the carrier so Telegraph and Signal could look out and get some air.

"Maybe this will make you happier, my darlings," she said lovingly to the kittens. Miss Splash put a little cup into the carrier. It was filled with dry kitten food.

"Oh, yummy," Signal said to Telegraph, as he took a bite of the food. Telegraph also ate some food and then curled up at the bottom of the carrier. "I'm very sleepy, Signal," she said with a yawn. "I think I'll take a nap. Maybe you should, too."

"All right," Signal agreed. "I'm tired, too."

Miss Splash pulled out a magazine and started reading, while the kittens fell fast asleep in the carrier.

As Miss Splash read and the kittens napped, a young boy sitting with his mother across the waiting room spied the carrier. "Look, Mom! That lady has a puppy or a kitten with her. May I go over and see it?" "Yes," replied his mother, "but be polite and don't ask if you can pick it up."

The little boy jumped out of his seat and ran over to Miss Splash. As he got closer, he saw there were two kittens in the carrier. Excitedly, he yelled back to his mother, "Mom, there are two kittens in there!" People in the waiting area looked over at Miss Splash and the carrier. The boy's mother smiled, put her finger to her lips, and mouthed, "*Use your inside voice, please!*"

Miss Splash smiled at the little boy who stood beaming in front of the kittens. "Those kittens are so, so plushy," he said. "They look like stuffed animals. What are their names? What kind are they?"

18

Signal pretended to ignore the little boy, but opened one eye to get a glimpse of him. Telegraph opened both eyes and gave the little boy a big smile to show off her cute little doll face.

"The one smiling at you is the little girl, Telegraph, and the sleeping one is Signal, the boy," said Miss Splash. "They are British Shorthair kittens. Do you know the Alice in Wonderland story?" she asked the boy, who nodded back. "...well, the Cheshire Cat in the story is a British Shorthair."

"She is so cute," said the little boy to Miss Splash. "I just love her chubby face."

Telegraph was enjoying all of the attention. She stood up and put her two front paws on the top of the carrier so the little boy could scratch her head.

"Humph," said Signal to himself. "All that fuss over a little round face. Miss Splash said I was a handsome kitty!"

Several other people in the waiting area overheard the little boy talking about the kittens. An older lady came over to see Telegraph and said to Miss Splash, "Oh, what an adorable kitten. I've never seen that breed before. She is so sweet." Miss Splash picked Telegraph up out of the carrier so the lady could see her better.

Signal opened his other eye and peeked up at the lady and the little boy who weren't paying any attention to him. "I guess no one cares about me. I might just as well sleep," he whispered to himself, although he knew Telegraph couldn't possibly hear him, with all the commotion she was causing.

Within a few minutes, a circle of people appeared around Miss Splash and Telegraph. Telegraph was showing off for the people, turning to the left and then to the right, so people could see her better. She soon forgot all about Signal in the carrier.

Signal's feelings were hurt. "Well, if she is going to get all the attention and no one is going to talk to me, I think I'll just get out of the carrier and find someplace quiet to sleep," Signal said to himself. "They'll never miss me."

Signal jumped out of the carrier and made a beeline for an open door leading down the jet way to a plane. At the end of the jet way, he saw a baby's car seat that was sitting by the door waiting to be loaded on the plane. It had a cover on it, but the zipper over the front was not closed all the way. "This looks cozy," Signal said, as he jumped into the seat and dove underneath the cover, so that he was completely covered up. "I'll just sleep here." In a few minutes, he was fast asleep and didn't see the gate agent close the door from the waiting room.

As Mr. Bubbles walked back to the waiting area, he was startled to see a large crowd of people gathered around Miss Splash. He beamed proudly, as he watched Miss Splash holding Telegraph so the people could see her, and chuckled as he heard them asking questions about the breed. He thought Signal must be sitting on Miss Splash's lap, and he was surprised that he wasn't there when he broke through the crowd to sit down next to Miss Splash.

"Our little Telegraph has created quite a stir," Mr. Bubbles said to Miss Splash. Mr. Bubbles had brought some water and he thought he'd offer it to Signal in the carrier. He reached over to the carrier next to Miss Splash and nearly dropped the water when he saw that Signal wasn't in the carrier! "Signal is missing!" he yelled in a loud voice.

The crowd around Miss Splash became silent and Miss Splash jumped up clutching Telegraph to her chest. "Missing!" she cried. "He was just there. Oh dear, where can he be?"

"Signal, you come back here," said Telegraph clearly annoyed that Signal was spoiling her time in the spotlight. "Stop playing games and come out!" she said in a loud voice.

After a few minutes when Signal didn't appear, Telegraph began to cry. "I'm sorry, Signal. Where are you? Please come back."

"Spread out, everyone, and look for the kitten," said a man to the crowd of people. They fanned out and started calling, "Signal, Signal, where are you?"

Miss Splash put Telegraph back in the carrier and zipped it up. Telegraph was making a terrible noise, as she was also calling, "Signal, Signal, where are you?"

Signal was oblivious to the frantic search taking place in the waiting area, since the jet way door was closed. He was sleeping so soundly that he didn't hear the baggage handler when he opened the little door to the ground and took the car seat down some stairs to a large conveyer belt. The conveyer belt was loaded with suitcases going into the storage compartment on a plane.

The baggage handler placed the car seat on the conveyer belt. Signal was still fast asleep.

Back in the waiting area, the little boy was visibly upset by Signal's disappearance. He ran around the waiting area searching every place he thought Signal might be hiding. He looked under all the seats, behind the ticket counter, and in the trash cans. No Signal. He ran so fast he was out of breath and stopped by the window to look at the plane.

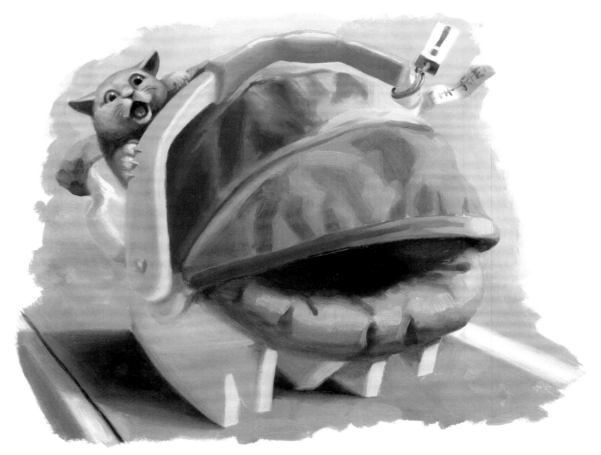

The baggage handler pushed a button, and the conveyer belt lurched forward with a jolt, startling Signal, who woke up and pushed his head out from under the car seat cover to see what was happening. "Oh my goodness," he cried aloud. "I'm on one of those big black moving things headed for a big dark hole. Help!" he screamed.

The little boy was fascinated by the moving luggage and pressed his face to the glass to get a better look. Suddenly, he spied Signal's little head poking out of the car seat.

Jumping up and down, he called, "There he is; there is Signal! He's going into that plane!"

Mr. Bubbles raced over to the window to get a better look. "He's there all right," said Mr. Bubbles. "Good eyes," he said, patting the boy's shoulder. "Now, if Signal will just stay in that car seat until we get him."

Miss Splash heard Telegraph meowing loudly from the carrier, but she ran over to the gate agent. "Our missing kitten is on the conveyer belt headed to the plane. Please, call someone fast!"

The gate agent picked up her microphone to call the baggage crew just about the same time the baggage man inside the plane caught a glimpse of Signal, who was yelling at the top of his lungs.

He stopped the conveyer belt and walked down towards the car seat. "How did you get here little kitty?" he said, as he reached down and carefully pulled Signal out. "You need to be in a carrier before you can come on a plane." Signal was so relieved to be off that car seat ride that he licked the man's face.

The crowd in the waiting area watched the whole scene. When Signal was rescued, they clapped and cheered. Miss Splash unzipped the carrier and bent down to hug Telegraph, who gave her a kiss. A tear fell from Miss Splash's face onto Telegraph's fur. "He's safe," she said, stroking Telegraph's head.

The baggage handler brought Signal into the waiting area and handed him to Mr. Bubbles. People gathered around him and cheered again. Everyone wanted to pet him.

"Are you OK, little guy?" Mr. Bubbles asked. "What a brave little boy you are. We were worried about you!"

"Hello, handsome," Miss Splash said, as she petted Signal and rubbed her face against his ears. From the carrier, Telegraph pushed against the mesh and said, "Signal, I was so worried. I'm sorry I was only thinking about myself and all the attention I was getting."

"Oh, that's OK," said Signal, enjoying his moment of glory. "I guess I was a little jealous, but it was nothing really," he said. He was thinking of how nice it was to see that obviously, everyone liked him, too.

Miss Splash put Signal in the carrier next to Telegraph, who licked his face and put her head on his paw. Before too long, everyone boarded the plane for the trip home.

By the time Mr. Bubbles pulled the car up to Friday Harbor, it had been a long day for all of them. Everyone was exhausted.

"I'm so glad we're home," Signal said to his sister. "We have been in this carrier for so long, and I can hardly wait to see our new house. I just want to meet Auntie Annie and go to sleep."

"Me, too," Telegraph yawned. "It is so dark we can't see the water, but I guess it will be there when we wake up tomorrow."

Miss Splash held the carrier, while Mr. Bubbles unlocked the front door. Inside, she set the carrier down carefully on the floor and unzipped the top so the kittens could jump out. "You are home my darlings," she said. "Auntie Annie!" she called. "Come meet the newest members of our family."

As Telegraph and Signal stepped carefully from the carrier and stretched their legs, Auntie Annie came around the corner and stopped to study the new kittens.

"Hello, my little doodlebugs," Auntie Annie said, as the kittens jumped at the sound of her voice. "Come over here and introduce yourselves to your new Auntie Annie. I've been waiting all day for you and was getting worried."

Telegraph was the first to approach Auntie Annie, prancing over to her and touching her shoulder with her paw. "I'm Telegraph," she stated confidently, "and I'm so pleased to meet you." Auntie Annie extended her paw and touched Telegraph on the face. "You are as cute as your pictures and I'm so glad you are here," she said.

Signal walked cautiously over to Auntie Annie and in his best-behavior voice said, "I'm Signal and it is nice to meet you." Then he started jumping around, as his words tumbled out. "I set off the alarm at the airport and got lost in the waiting area and went up on the moving thing into a plane and our plane was three hours late and everyone was worried and, and……"

"Slow down, Signal," Auntie Annie said. "My goodness, you had an adventure for such a little fellow! You'll have to tell me all about it tomorrow. It is late and you need to get to bed."

Auntie Annie led the kittens into the family room where two soft, round beds had been placed next to Auntie Annie's rocking chair. Signal barely slid into his bed before his eyes closed, and he started making purring noises.

"He always goes to sleep first," said Telegraph, who hopped into her bed and snuggled into a tight ball. "Oh, Auntie Annie, I know we are going to be so happy here," she said. "Thank you for waiting up for us, I………." Telegraph never finished her sentence, as she was fast asleep.

Auntie Annie looked lovingly at the two little kittens and gave each one of them a quick lick on the face. She climbed into her rocking chair and thought about how busy things would be now. All the outside animals at Friday Harbor were eager to meet the new kittens. They had waited all day with her, but when the kittens didn't come home before bedtime, Auntie Annie had sent the animals home. In the morning, Henrietta, the white duck, would tap on the window, as she did every day.

Auntie Annie smiled to herself. She thought of how she would tell Telegraph and Signal the many tales of Friday Harbor.

"Goodnight, my little doodlebugs," she whispered. "Sweet dreams, dance on bright moon beams, and be ready for your new adventures."

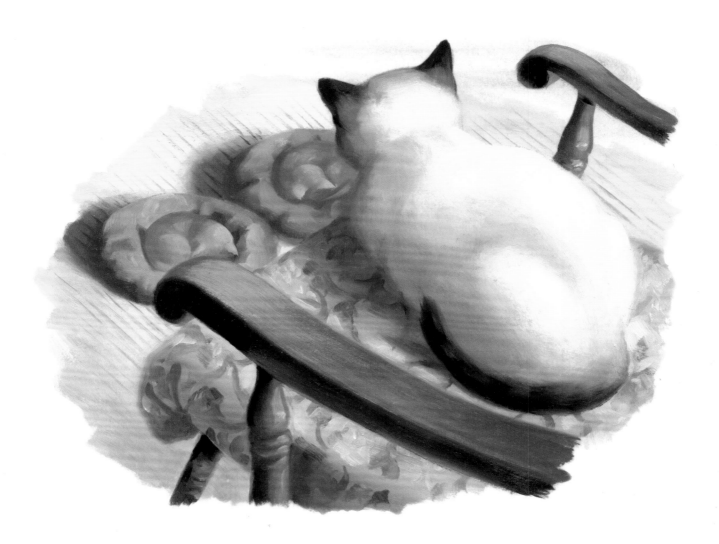